The Cat in the Coconut Hat

C.J. Gillett
Illustrated by Juan Sebastián Amadeo

For my parents, Charles M. Gillett and Sarita Gabourel-Gillett,
who always encouraged me to pursue my dreams.
Special thanks to Sara Silverman, Danielle Poiesz
at Double Vision Editorial, Kendra Archer, all my early supporters on
Patreon, and also my fellow Belizeans! I could not have
made this book without each and every one of you.

This book belongs to

....

....

....

There once was a very curious but cautious little cat who lived on a small island just off the coast of Belize.

Every day before the sun was hot, the little cat would wake up and walk along the beach in search of food.

"Dah weh ah wah eat tideh?"
"What am I going to eat today?"

Almost every night, Belizeans would boat out to his island with bags of food and legs that were ready to dance the night away.

The local singers and musicians would fill the air with all different types of tropical music—from Punta Rock to Calypso, and Reggae to Brukdown music.

Everyone would dance and dance!

Just before the roosters crowed, the Belizeans would depart the island and leave behind whatever food they could not eat. Fresh red snapper, juicy lobsters, and even jumbo shrimp were often left for the cat to scavenge. There was always something delicious to eat.

One morning, the cat woke up to the sound of a boat coming to shore.

When a little girl hopped out of the boat, the cat ran and hid behind a nearby mangrove tree.

He watched as she walked along the beach searching for and picking up garbage and food that the previous night's visitors had left behind.

"Noh, man! Noh tek mi food, gyal!"
"Noooo! Don't take my food, girl!"

But the little girl did not listen.

Raising his paws in desperation, the cat finally screamed,
"Luk, ya gyal! Noh touch mi food! Dis dah fi me!"
"Look here, girl! This is my food! Leave it alone! It's mine!"

The little girl turned toward the cat and smiled.
"Good morning, Mr. Cat!"

"Tcho!" the cat replied while pounding his paws on the sand.
"Argh!"

"Dis dah mi food! Lef it lone, noh, gyal!"
"This is my food! Leave it alone, girl!"

The cat was very proud that he was
standing up for himself,
but the girl went back to picking up
the garbage as if she hadn't heard him.

Shocked and in disbelief, the cat watched as the little girl filled up her bags and took them back to her boat. "I'll be back tomorrow!" she said as she waved goodbye.

"Timaaro? Wy? Fi wat? Shucks mein! Noh kohn bak timaaro, yuh hear, or yuh wah regret it fi true," the cat replied.

"Tomorrow? Why? What for? Don't come back tomorrow, you hear, or you are going to regret it!"

After she was gone, the cat ran up and down the beach looking for all his favorite foods.

But there was no food to be found.

That day his belly
rumbled with hunger.

GRRRRRR

When the next day arrived
and the night's visitors had all
departed, the cat quickly collected his meal.

With his belly full, the cat sprawled out across the white, gleaming sand.

"Now dis dah livin' fi true!" yawned the cat.
"Now this is the life!"

Then he laid his head down on a hammock he had
made out of some plastic wrappings.

Everything was peaceful and back to normal.
Soon he was fast asleep.

Later that morning, however, a heavy rumbling shook the entire beach and awoke the cat from his peaceful slumber.

"Dah weh di goh aan?" he wondered out loud.
"What is going on?"

The cat grabbed all the food next to him as fast as he possibly could and hid behind a nearby coconut tree.

"Mosi dah lee gyal di kohn bak fi tek mi food!"
"It must be that little girl coming back to take my food!"

Looking out at the water, the cat saw that the rumbling was not coming from the little girl. Instead, there were many people wearing silly hats and holding shovels and axes. Some were even driving heavy machinery!

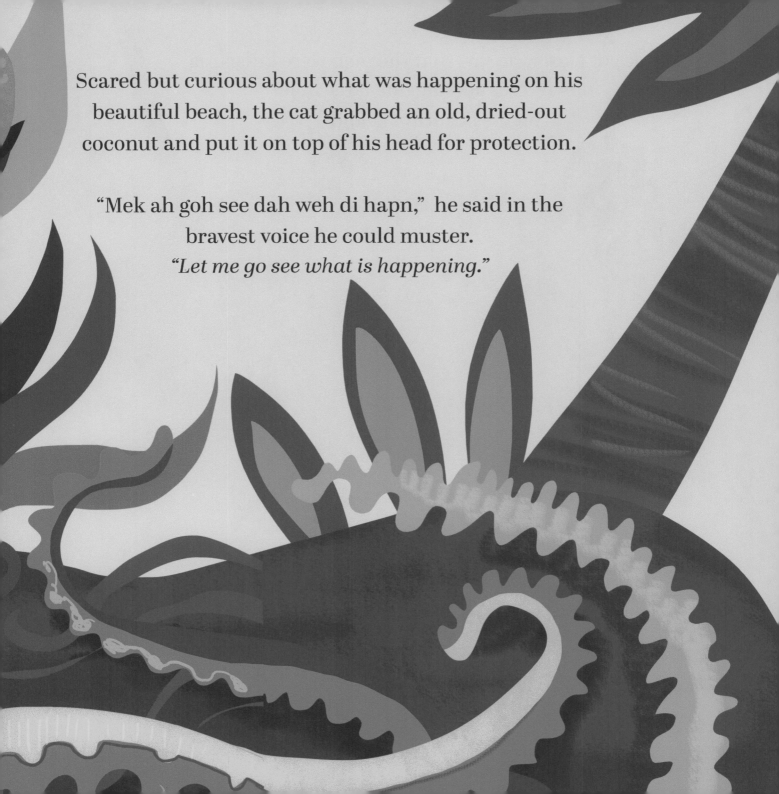

Scared but curious about what was happening on his beautiful beach, the cat grabbed an old, dried-out coconut and put it on top of his head for protection.

"Mek ah goh see dah weh di hapn," he said in the bravest voice he could muster.
"Let me go see what is happening."

As he got closer, he saw that the men were knocking
down trees and digging large holes
on his beautiful island.

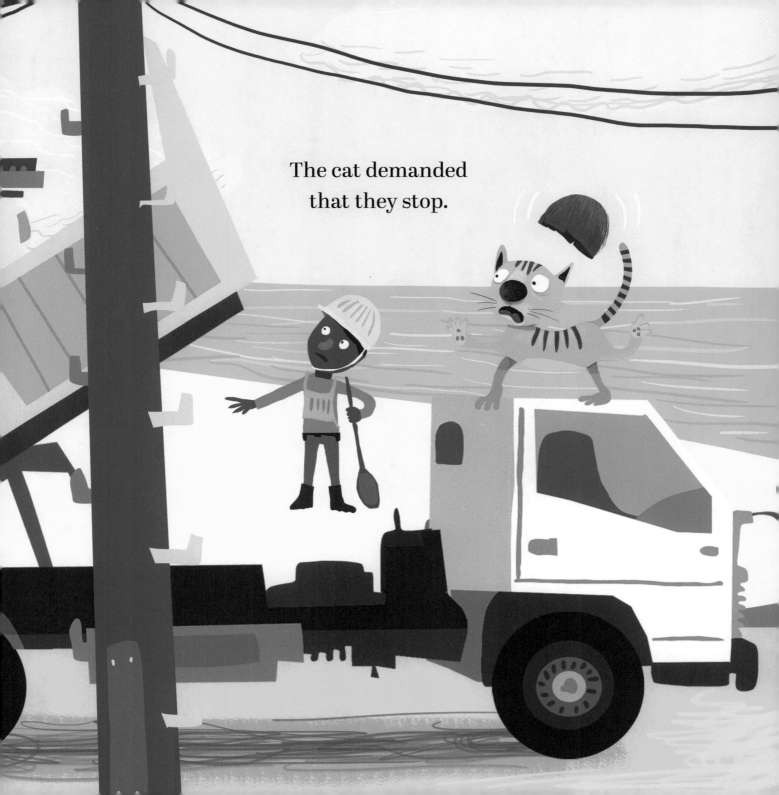

The cat demanded
that they stop.

All the cat had ever known and loved was being destroyed,
and there was nothing he could do about it.

Later that day, the little girl returned to the island.

She came over to the cat and picked him up, surprising him.

"You know what, Mr. Cat?" she started. "This is no place for a kitty like you. I asked my parents, and they said I can bring you home with me! Would you like that?"

Feeling like he had no other choice, the cat went off in the boat with the little girl.

They watched his island grow smaller and smaller as they sailed away.

When the boat reached the mainland of Belize
and pulled into the dock, the cat and the little
girl were greeted by an older man and woman
with wide grins on their faces.

"Welcome home, Mr. Cat," they said as they handed him a bowl full of fresh fruit and fish. Hesitantly, the cat slowly approached the food.

His home had been destroyed. He was in a new place.

But somehow, he felt calm with this new family.
It was something he could get used to.

When night fell, however, the cat had trouble sleeping.

While he was grateful to the family for welcoming him, he missed the protection of the coconut trees. He missed the sound of the waves crashing against the beach. He missed the smell of the sweet ocean breeze.

So he snuck away to the coast of Belize city to make himself a new home.

And that is how the cat in the coconut hat
arrived on the shores of Belize.

If dah noh soh, dah naily soh.

*If that's not how it happened, it's close to
how it happened.*

C.J. Gillett

C.J. Gillett is of Belizean heritage and grew up in New York City. He currently resides in Pittsburgh, PA, where he writes children's stories and works as a practicing physical therapist. He hopes to inspire young writers of diverse backgrounds to explore the fantastic world of children's literature and share their own cultural stories. Find him at booksbycjgillett.com.

Juan Sebastián Amadeo

Born in Avellaneda, Buenos Aires, Juan is a self-taught illustrator, plastic artist, and muralist. For over fifteen years, he has specialized in children's literature illustrations working for publishers all over the world. His works have been published in over twelve countries. He is currently a member of the London-based international illustrator's agency Allied Artist.
Check out his work on Instagram at @juansebastionamadeo.

CPSIA information can be obtained
at www.ICGtesting.com
Printed in the USA
LVHW070050201120
672011LV00002B/50

* 9 7 8 1 7 3 4 9 4 6 3 0 7 *